THE ANT
and the ELEPHANT

written and illustrated by BILL PEET

Houghton Mifflin Company Boston

LIBRARY OF CONGRESS CATALOG CARD NO. 74-179918
ISBN: 0-395-16963-1 REINFORCED EDITION
ISBN: 0-395-29205-0 SANDPIPER PAPERBOUND EDITION
PRINTED IN THE UNITED STATES OF AMERICA
WOZ   30 29 28 27 26 25 24 23

One morning a tiny ant crawled up a tall blade of jungle grass for
a view of the river. All at once he was caught by a breeze that sent
him sailing off into the swirling water. Just when it seemed he would
be swept downstream and gone forever, the ant grabbed onto a snag
and scrambled to safety.

There the ant remained stranded wondering what he would do, when he spied a mud turtle creeping along the riverbank.

"Oh, Mr. Hardshell!" called the ant in his wee, small voice. "Would you be so kind as to give me a lift back to dry land? It's a nice day for a swim."

The old turtle turned his head slowly. After a long look at the ant, he said, "I've had my swim for today, and besides, if I went racing about helping everyone who was in trouble I'd have no time left to relax." Then the turtle tottered on his way to find a place where he could sun himself.

When the turtle came to a flat, warm rock, he crept slowly up the edge. Suddenly he went toppling backward and landed upside down. "Blast it all," he muttered. "Dad blame it!" And he began thrash-

ing out with his legs, desperately trying to right himself. But all the kicking could do was to send him rocking about on his shell. That was all.

As he stretched his stringy neck looking about for help, the turtle spied a hornbill roosting on her nest high on a tree limb.

"Oh, Mrs. Bigbill!" he called. "Would you mind helping me back to my feet? With one flip of your beak I'm sure you could do it."

"I could," snapped the bird, "but I won't. This will teach you not to be so clumsy."

As she leaned down to say more, the hornbill tipped the nest and
her one big egg rolled out to go tumbling all the way to the ground.
Luckily it landed in a clump of fluff-twuff weeds without so much as
a crack.

"Thank goodness," she cried, when she found the egg all in one piece. Then, seizing it in her beak, she fluttered her wings as she tried to take off. But her oversized beak plus the cumbersome egg were too much of a load. Still she kept on furiously thrashing the air until her wings were worn to a frazzle.

As the miserable bird sat there staring helplessly at the egg, a giraffe came striding along.

"Oh, Mr. Greatneck!" she called. "You've come just at the right time. If I perched on your head with the egg in my beak, you could carry us back up to my nest."

"Indeed no!" scoffed the proud giraffe. "If I did such a thing how silly I would look. I'll have no one laughing at me. No, indeed!" And Mr. Greatneck went on his way with his head held high, nibbling at the treetops.

He was so intent upon the tasty leaves he didn't notice the tangle-dangle vine until it was twisted up around one leg.

"Here now!" snorted the giraffe with an angry kick. "How dare you!" The kick merely gave the vine an extra twist which tightened

its grip. Then in a fury the giraffe began kicking wildly about with all four legs. The more he kicked the more entangled he became. Finally, his legs were so tightly tied up in the vine he couldn't budge.

As he stood there in the tangle, he spied a lion heading his way.

"What good luck," thought the giraffe. "With those great claws of his he could rip this vine to shreds in one swipe."

"Oh, Mr. Bigpaw!" he called to the lion. "Just look at me!"

The lion took one look, then burst into a great roaring laugh. "Ho! Ho! That is funny. Ho! Ho! I see what you mean. Ho! Ho! Ho!" And, laughing merrily, he went on his way through the jungle.

The lion was still laughing to himself as he flopped down in a patch of shade for a bit of a catnap. He flopped down with such a *whump!* it upset a huge boulder which was all set to topple. To the lion's surprise it rolled over and came down right upon his tail.

With a furious roar he leaped to his feet, tugging frantically to free himself. But he soon found it was useless to struggle. He could never get loose unless he was willing to part with his tail.

As he sat there growling over his bad luck, a rhino came along.

"Oh, Mr. Hornyhead!" he called. "Would you mind bumping this stupid boulder off my tail? One nudge of your great snout would do it."

"I would," said the rhino, "if you could think of some way to return the favor."

"Right now," sighed the lion, "all I can think of is my poor tail."

"Too bad," said the rhino, and he went lumbering off through the trees.

The rhino never bothered to watch where he was going. With a
great horn out front he went plowing straight ahead through the

brambles and brush, when all of a sudden *zump!*—he blundered
head-on into a stump with his great horn stuck deep into it.

"Out of my way, you stupid stump!" He snorted. And with a furious lunge he tried to knock over the stump. This drove the horn still deeper. Then with a mighty tug he tried pulling himself free, but the stump refused to let go. At last the rhino realized he was hopelessly stuck.

So the rhino, the lion, the giraffe, the hornbill, the turtle, and the ant were left in deep trouble. That would have been that if a jolly big somebody hadn't decided to take a stroll through the jungle that day.

It was a huge elephant with such great spreading ears he could hear the slightest sound—the faint rustle of a leaf, the least snap of a twig, or even the tiny voice of an ant calling.

He reached his long trunk out over the river, inviting the ant to climb aboard, then carried him safely back to dry land.

"How can I ever thank you enough!" cried the grateful ant.

"It was no big thing," said the elephant.

"But it was a big thing for me," said the ant. "It was everything!" And he scurried away through the grass.

"If you've got time to bother with a nothing of an ant," grumbled the old turtle, "how about me?"

"You *are* in a pickle," said the elephant, and with the tip of his trunk he flipped the turtle back onto his feet.

Then without a word of thanks the old codger went tottering away down the bank to disappear in the river.

"If you can help an ugly old turtle," squawked the hornbill, "the least you can do is put my lovely egg back in the nest."

"The very least I can do," agreed the elephant, and holding the

egg gently in his trunk, he carried it up to the nest.

"It's a wonder you didn't crack it," snapped the bird, as she settled down onto the egg.

"Say now," chuckled the elephant, when he came upon the giraffe, "that's what I call a funny fix."

"Not funny to me!" snorted the giraffe. "Not one bit funny!"

"Then I'll try not to laugh," said the big fellow, searching through the vine with his trunk to get at the worst of the tangle.

It took a few minutes to undo the dozens of knots that gripped the long legs. Once they were loose, the vine fell limply to the ground.

"Well, I must say, it's about time," snorted the snooty giraffe, as he went gallopity-clopping away.

"What have we here?" asked the elephant, when he came to the lion.

"We have a big, stupid, bumbling boulder," growled the lion. "That's what!"

"Then be off, stupid boulder!" And the huge tusker heaved the boulder into the air with his trunk and sent it tumbling.

Once he was free, the lion gave his tail a few switches to make sure it was working. "What a relief," sighed the lion. "Someday when I'm in a better mood I must remember to thank you."

"No hurry," said the elephant.

He continued on his way through the jungle, where he soon found the hopelessly stuck rhino.

"I can pull you free," said the elephant, "if your tail can stand one mighty tug."

"Right now it's my snout I'm worried about," groaned the rhino, "so jerk away!"

Gripping the rhino's tail tightly in his trunk, the elephant reared

back, and with one almighty jerk the rhino went sailing free of the stump to land with one big *blump!*

"That was one whale of a jerk," muttered the rhino. "I hope you got some fun out of it."

"It was a pleasure," smiled the elephant, as he went merrily on his way.

He was enormously pleased with himself after all the good deeds he had done that day.

"Everyone has his troubles." He chuckled. "Everyone but big me. I'll never get into a fix where I need help. That's one thing for sure." The elephant didn't suspect there was a deep ravine just ahead. It was too well hidden by scatter-flat ferns.

Before he knew it, he had tumbled straight into it, landing with a seven-ton *thud* that shook the whole jungle. He was wedged so deep and in such a position that his trunk and his legs were useless.

"It serves me right," he muttered, "for feeling so almighty big and all powerful. Now I'm the one who needs help.

"Help!" he bellowed. "Help! Help! Help!" Then he waited anxiously for a reply. He waited for hours, staring up at the sky until it faded into evening and a deep stillness settled over the jungle.

It was so quiet his great spreading ears caught the sound of footsteps—tiny, tiny footsteps from somewhere above.

"Who's there?" asked the elephant.

"It's me," said a wee, small voice. "The ant you rescued this morning and all my ant friends. Ninety-five thousand of them."

"I know ants are amazingly strong," said the elephant, "but surely you don't expect to lift me out of here."

"We can try," said the ant. "Come on, my friends, let's get to work."

Suddenly down the steep wall of the ravine came a teeming horde of ants swarming under the elephant. Then all together they began chanting, "Heave ho! Heave ho! Up you go! Up you go!" And to the elephant's amazement he felt himself moving upward. Slowly but surely, just an inch at a time, the tireless ants hoisted their huge burden up the wall.

"Heave ho! Up you go! Don't lose your grip! Don't anyone trip!"
And at last, under a bright full moon they set the elephant down in
the scatter-flat ferns.

"That was tremendous!" cried the elephant. "I can't believe it!"

"It was nothing," replied the ninety-five thousand ants.

"Nothing for you," said the elephant, "but a mighty big thing for
me. Now if you'll climb aboard I'll give you a ride back to your ant
hill."

"I'm not a bit tired," said one ant, "but I would like a ride. I've never ridden on an elephant."

"Neither have I," cried all the others, and they swarmed up the elephant's legs onto his back. Then away they went herumpity-bumpity clumpity-hump—the mighty big and the mighty small, off through the jungle together.